For Amir —MB

For Sylvie —GP

VIKING

An imprint of Penguin Random House LLC, New York

First published in the United States of America by Viking,
an imprint of Penguin Random House LLC, 2020

LIBRARY OF CONGRESS CATALOGING-IN-PUBLICATION DATA IS AVAILABLE
ISBN 9780593113820

Manufactured in China
Book design by Greg Pizzoli and Jim Hoover   Set in Clarion MT Pro

10   9   8   7   6   5   4   3   2   1

JACK AT BAT

Mac Barnett & Greg Pizzoli

Viking

1.

GAME DAY

It is the big game.
The Lady Town Ladies
play the Big City Brats.

Let's root for the Ladies!

Not for the Brats!

The Lady
will pitch.

Rex plays
left field.

Jack is the bat boy.

He picks up the bats.

Don't swing that bat, Jack!

Jack! Drop that bat.

Good. Now pick it back up.

That's what you do, Jack.
You pick up bats.

"Play ball!"
cries the ump.

Let's beat the Brats!

2.

AN HOUR GOES BY

The bases are loaded.
The Brats are at bat.

The Lady throws
a fastball.

A Brat bashes it back.

A big hit to left field!
Rex runs after it.

Good Rex!
Fetch that ball, Rex!

Yes! Fetch it, Rex.

Oh no. Rex runs
the wrong way.

The ball's in his mouth.
Rex runs to the stands.

He runs out
of the park.

Rex, "fetch" means
bring it back!

The Brats round the bases.

But wait, where's home plate?
The Brats can't score if they
don't touch home plate.

And home plate is gone.
It should be right there.
Right next to the ump.

Right next to Jack.

Jack, what's that
in your shirt?

That weird shape, Jack.
That home-plate-shaped
thing in your shirt, Jack.

Jack, put it down.
Put home plate down, Jack.
We don't want to cheat.
Be a good sport, Jack.

That's four runs for the Brats.

3.

JACK'S DREAM

Two more hours go by.
Jack takes a nap in
the stands.

In his dream,
Jack swings a bat.

Don't swing that bat, Jack!
Don't swing that bat!

Not even in dreams, Jack.
Don't swing that bat!

Your swing is too wild.
Your swing is too fast.

You are the bat boy.
You just pick up the bats.

4.

WE NEED JACK

The game has picked up!
The Ladies came back!

Well, sort of.

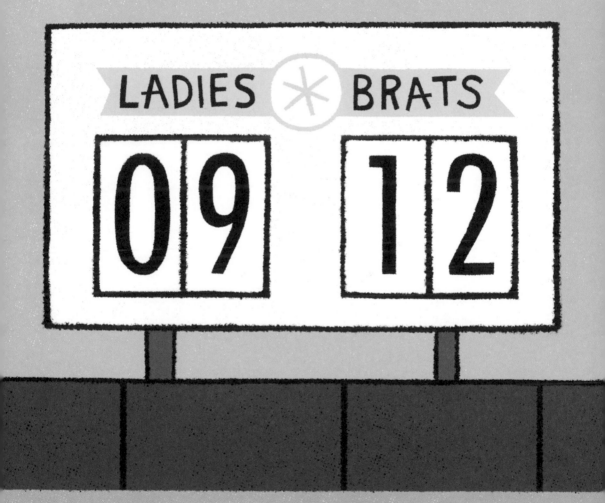

The comeback took place
while Jack took a nap.

It's the ninth!
(That's the end.)
We need four
runs to win!

The bases are loaded.
There are two outs.

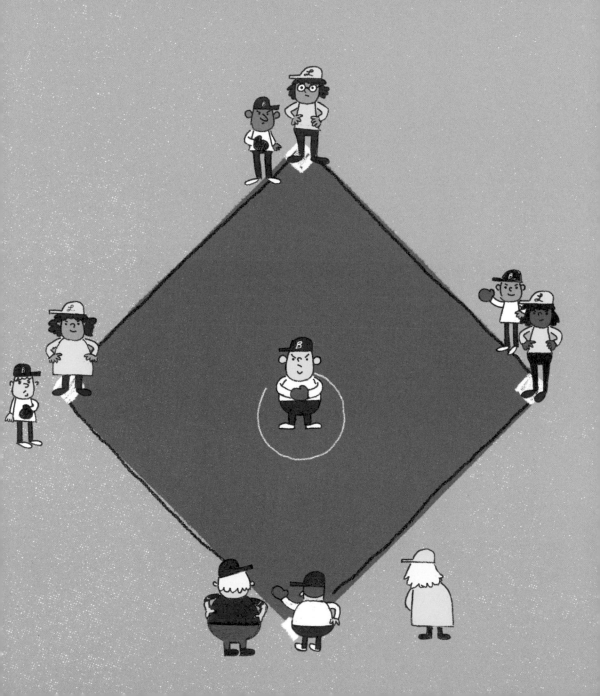

We need a pinch hit.
(A "pinch" is a tight spot,
and that's what we're in.)
We need a home run.

Hey!

Let's call Jack in.

Wake up, Jack!
Wake up! Wake up!
Wake up, Jack!

It's all up to you, Jack!
Jack, pick up a bat.
We need you to swing, Jack.
Swing wild! Swing fast!

Jack picks up the bat.
Jack walks to the plate.
Jack points to the stands.
That means, "I will hit
a home run."

Jack, you should not do that.
You should not brag, Jack.

(Still, that was cool, Jack.
It was kind of cool to point
to the stands.)

The pitch!

A fastball!

A swing and a miss!
Strike one.

The fans gasp.

The pitch!

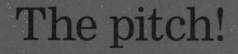

A curveball!

A swing and a miss.

That is strike two.
Wow! This is tense!

A big swing.

CRACK!

Jack breaks his bat.
It's a smash hit!

The ball flies to the stands!
That's a home run!
You did it, Jack!

Now run round the bases!
That's good! That's good, Jack!

The team waits at home plate
to give hugs and high fives.
Run to home plate, Jack!
Come home, Jack!

Oh no. Cracker Jacks.

Don't let Jack
see those snacks!

Don't run for those
snacks, Jack!

Just touch home plate, Jack!
Then the Ladies will win!
Jack, please come back!

OK. Jack's not coming back.
He won't leave those snacks.

So . . . that means it's a tie!
The Ladies tie the Brats!

Everyone loves a tie, right?

In a way, we all win?

Right?

IF YOU WANT MORE JACK, READ: